Amelia Bedelia, Rocket Scientist?

BY HERMAN PARISH

PICTURES BY LYNN SWEAT

SCHOLASTIC INC.

NEW YORK TORONTO LONDON AUCKLAND SYDNEY
MEXICO CITY NEW DELHI HONG KONG BUENOS AIRES

ISBN 0-439-79907-4

Text copyright © 2005 by Herman S. Parish III.
Illustrations copyright © 2005 by Lynn Sweat.
All rights reserved. Published by
Scholastic Inc., 557 Broadway, New York, NY 10012,
by arrangement with Greenwillow Books,
an imprint of HarperCollins Publishers.
SCHOLASTIC and associated logos are trademarks
and/or registered trademarks of Scholastic Inc.

12 11 10 9 8 7 6 5 4 3 2 1   6 7 8 9 10 11/0

Printed in the U.S.A.   23

First Scholastic paperback printing, September 2006

Watercolor and black pen were used to prepare the full-color art.

The text type is Times.

For Philip,
the original "Happy Man"—H. P.

To my sisters,
Evelyn and Betty—L. S.

"**T**his is incredible," said Mr. Rogers.

"Who is the rocket scientist

who put my glasses in the dishwasher?"

"I am," said Amelia Bedelia.

"Thank you for promoting me.

You told me to wash all of the glasses."

"Wait just a minute," said Mr. Rogers.

"Reading glasses are different."

"Sorry," said Amelia Bedelia,

"I cannot wait a second.

Miss Edwards, the science teacher,

needs my help at the science fair."

"Science?" said Mr. Rogers.

"You don't know anything about science."

Amelia Bedelia was too far away to hear.

"Wait," he called out. "You forgot your—"

Amelia Bedelia arrived at the school.

"Mr. Rogers is so thoughtful,"

she said to herself.

"He promoted me from housekeeper

to rocket scientist

just in time for the science fair."

"Wow," said Amelia Bedelia.

"Look at all these amazing projects.

Miss Edwards makes science

such fun."

"Hi, Miss Edwards," said Amelia Bedelia.

"Happy science fair."

"Same to you," said Miss Edwards.

"I'm so glad you volunteered to help."

"Sorry I am late," said Amelia Bedelia.

"Mr. Rogers called my work incredible,

and then he promoted me."

"Congratulations," said Miss Edwards.

"I just got here, too. I was in a make-up test."

"You should get an A," said Amelia Bedelia.

"Your lipstick looks great."

"It was not for me," said Miss Edwards.

"The make-up test was for my students."

"Are you kidding?" said Amelia Bedelia.

"These children are way too young

to wear makeup."

"I agree," said Miss Edwards.

"The only things they had to make up

were the answers."

"What a big kid!" said Amelia Bedelia.

"He is a judge," said Miss Edwards.

"A judge?" said Amelia Bedelia.

"Shouldn't he be in court?"

"Not quite," said Miss Edwards.

"He is judging our science fair.

He is a famous scientist.

I invited him from the university."

"Amelia Bedelia," said Miss Edwards,

"I would like you to meet Dr. Dinglebatt."

"Hello there," said the man.

"I am Don Dinglebatt, professor."

"Pleased to meet you," said Amelia Bedelia.

"I am Amelia Bedelia, rocket scientist."

"Oh, really?" said Dr. Dinglebatt.

"Yes, really," said Amelia Bedelia.

"I also keep house for Mrs. Rogers."

"Housekeeping?" said Dr. Dinglebatt.

"You call that rocket science?"

"Not me," said Amelia Bedelia.

"That's what Mr. Rogers calls it."

"Good for you," said Dr. Dinglebatt.

"It sounds like Mr. Rogers

respects the work you do."

"Yes," said Miss Edwards.

"And your job, Dr. Dinglebatt,

is to judge every science project."

"Yes, indeed," said Dr. Dinglebatt.

"When I see the winner

I will shout 'Eureka!'"

"What is a eureka?" said Amelia Bedelia.

Miss Edwards shrugged and said,

"It is Greek to me."

"It is Greek to everyone,"

said Dr. Dinglebatt.

"In ancient Greece, a famous scientist

named Archimedes shouted 'Eureka!'

when he made a discovery in the bath."

"I get it," said Amelia Bedelia.

"*Eureka* means 'Ouch, this water is hot!'"

"No, it doesn't," said Dr. Dinglebatt.

"*Eureka* means 'I have found it.'"

"Found what?" asked Miss Edwards.

"The soap," said Amelia Bedelia.

"No, no, no!" said Dr. Dinglebatt.

"It means 'I found the answer.'"

A boy interrupted them.

"Excuse me," said Jason.

"I wanted to let you know that

a volcano will erupt in ten minutes."

"Take cover!" yelled Amelia Bedelia.

Jason laughed and said,

"Relax, this volcano is just a model."

"Is it safe now?"

said Amelia Bedelia.

"All clear," said Miss Edwards.

"I am glad to see that you take

this science fair so seriously.

You can assist Dr. Dinglebatt.

Right now I have to help Emily

set up her homemade telescope."

"Okay, Jason," said Dr. Dinglebatt.

"Let's test-drive your volcano."

They did not get very far.

"Hey, Jason," said Wendy.

"Would you help me get my saucer?

I hooked up my dad's leaf blower

to show how a flying saucer flies."

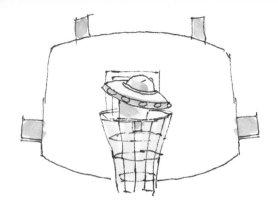

"Where is the cup?" said Amelia Bedelia.

"Flying saucers do not come

with their own teacups," said Dr. Dinglebatt.

"I see," said Amelia Bedelia,

"but I don't see a saucer."

"It is stuck up there,"

said Wendy.

"What a shame," said Amelia Bedelia.

"Would my bonnet work instead?"

"It might," said Wendy.

"Give it a try," said Dr. Dinglebatt.

"You are the rocket scientist."

Amelia Bedelia counted down:

"Five, four, three, two, one . . . blastoff!"

Wendy turned on the blower.

WHIR-R-R-R-RRR

Up, up, up went the bonnet.

"We have liftoff!" said Dr. Dinglebatt.

As Amelia Bedelia moved the blower,

her bonnet flew around and around.

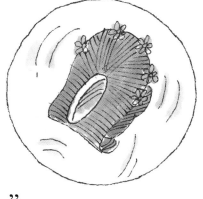

On the other side of the gym,

Emily shouted, "Look! It's a UFO!"

Miss Edwards focused the telescope.

"No, it isn't," she said.

"That flying object

is not unidentified.

It belongs to Amelia Bedelia.

I must go see what's going on."

"This is great," said Amelia Bedelia.

"It isn't scientific," said Dr. Dinglebatt.

"What fun," said Amelia Bedelia.

"UFOs don't exist," said Dr. Dinglebatt.

"Wheeeee!" said Amelia Bedelia.

"I am the judge," said Dr. Dinglebatt.

"I deserve a turn . . .

uh, I mean, to test it."

Dr. Dinglebatt reached for the blower.

He turned it off by mistake.

Amelia Bedelia's bonnet fell to earth.

"Look out below," said Amelia Bedelia.

"I had better get my bonnet

before it becomes another project."

She ran over to the next aisle.

27

"Eureka!" shouted Amelia Bedelia.

Dr. Dinglebatt came running.

"What is it?" he said.

"Did you find a winner?"

"No," said Amelia Bedelia.

"I found my bonnet.

Look where it landed!"

"A fellow housekeeper," said Dr. Dinglebatt.

"What a neat robot," said Amelia Bedelia.

"That is the whole idea," said Artie.

"My mom wants my room to be neat."

"Your mother is right," said Dr. Dinglebatt.

"I know," said Artie. "She always says,

'Pick up your room, pick up your room!'"

"That is impossible," said Amelia Bedelia.

"Your room must weigh a ton!

You could never pick up the bed,

the rug, the desk . . ."

"I believe," said Dr. Dinglebatt,

"that Artie's mother wants him

to pick up all the things on his floor:

his toys, his books, his clothes . . ."

"Oh, I see," said Amelia Bedelia.

"No wonder you are a professor."

Dr. Dinglebatt smiled and said,

"Okay, Artie, let's see Randy in action."

"Here is how he works," said Artie.

"I put little pieces of metal on all my stuff.

Then I put magnets on my robot's hands."

"So," continued Artie, "if I leave my stuff

on the floor, I can turn on Randy . . ."

"Presto—all picked up.

My mom is happy."

"Bravo!" said Dr. Dinglebatt.

"You are a first-rate inventor."

"Thanks," said Artie.

"Randy still has a few bugs in him."

"I can fix that," said Amelia Bedelia.

"Shoo!" said Amelia Bedelia.

"I'm warning you bugs.

Get out of Randy right now."

"Be careful," joked Dr. Dinglebatt.

"That contraption might replace you.

Imagine an army of housekeeping robots."

"That is scary," said Amelia Bedelia.

"Yoo-hoo," Miss Edwards called out.

Amelia Bedelia jumped.

"Hey," said Amelia Bedelia,

"don't scare me like that."

"Well, well," said Miss Edwards.

"I was worried that you two

might not be getting along."

"We get along fine,"

said Dr. Dinglebatt.

"So I see,"

said Miss Edwards.

YIPES!

35

"Look at the time," said Amelia Bedelia.

"We don't want to miss the volcano."

"I'm afraid I will," said Miss Edwards.

"Emily and her telescope still need help."

"See you later?" said Dr. Dinglebatt.

Miss Edwards just walked away.

"I think she is mad," said Dr. Dinglebatt.

"I don't blame her," said Amelia Bedelia.

 I would hate to miss an erupting volcano."

"I'll meet you there," said Dr. Dinglebatt.

"I need to look at some other projects."

"Hi, Jason," said Amelia Bedelia.

"When does your volcano erupt?"

"Never," said Jason.

"I have run out of baking soda."

Amelia Bedelia reached into her purse.

"You are in luck," said Amelia Bedelia.

"I just did a lot of baking.

I bought an extra box at the store."

"Oh, thank you, thank you," said Jason.

"One day I will win the Nobel Prize."

"Why no bell?" said Amelia Bedelia.

"Do they give buzzers instead?"

"No," said Jason. "The Nobel Prize

is the most important award in science."

"I hope you win it," said Amelia Bedelia.

"Show me how your volcano works."

"Step one," said Jason.

"Add a little bit of baking soda . . .

Step two: add some vinegar . . .

Uh-oh. I ran out of that, too."

"I can't help you,"

said Amelia Bedelia.

"Maybe the cafeteria

can spare some vinegar."

"Good idea," said Jason.

"I'll be right back."

"This volcano is amazing,"

said Amelia Bedelia to herself.

"Jason worked so hard on his project.

I hope Dr. Dinglebatt is impressed, too."

Amelia Bedelia had an idea.

She poured the rest of the baking soda

into the volcano.

"Saved again," said Jason.

"A nice cafeteria lady

loaned me some vinegar."

Just then Dr. Dinglebatt arrived.

"Looks like I am just in time," he said.

"You sure are," said Jason.

"Would you pour in the vinegar?"

"Sure," said Dr. Dinglebatt.

"It would be an honor."

The lava began to bubble.

Jason put on the top.

"Watch this," he said.

The volcano rumbled loudly.

"Is that normal?" said Wendy.

The volcano rocked and rolled.

"Is something wrong?" said Artie.

"Hmmm," said Amelia Bedelia.

"Maybe I should not have dumped in

that whole box of baking soda."

"A whole box?" said Dr. Dinglebatt.

"Run!" yelled Jason. "It's about to—"

"Gangway!" said Amelia Bedelia.

"This blower will blow it away."

WHIR-R-R-R

went the blower.

WHOOOOSH went

Dr. Dinglebatt's hair.

Miss Edwards heard the commotion

from across the gym.

She looked through the telescope.

"Gracious," said Miss Edwards.

"Now *that* is a UFO.

I'd better get over there."

"My hair!" said Dr. Dinglebatt.

The children pointed and laughed.

Amelia Bedelia turned off the blower.

The hairpiece fell back to earth.

"Eeeeek!" screamed a girl.

"A rat is attacking the mouse!"

Dr. Dinglebatt scooped up his hair.

"Excuse me, young lady," he said.

"This rat is going back to my lab."

Eeeeek!

Amelia Bedelia was just as upset.

"It's all my fault," she said.

"I was trying to help Jason

win the Nobel Prize."

"Nobel Prize?" said Dr. Dinglebatt.

"This deserves the dumbbell prize!"

Dr. Dinglebatt stalked out of the gym.

"He is a mad scientist," said Jason.

"You mean he is crazy?" said Artie.

"Like you see in horror movies?"

"No," said Wendy. "He is angry."

"He sure is," said Amelia Bedelia.

"When he found his hair,

he forgot to say 'Eureka!'"

"What happened?" said Miss Edwards.

Amelia Bedelia explained everything.

"How embarrassing," said Miss Edwards.

"Dr. Dinglebatt had a bad hair day."

"Worse than that," said Amelia Bedelia,

"he had a no hair day."

"Worst of all," said Miss Edwards.

"Our science fair has no winner."

"I feel terrible," said Amelia Bedelia.

"I ruined Jason's project.

I embarrassed Dr. Dinglebatt.

I don't feel like a rocket scientist.

I am going back to housekeeping."

Amelia Bedelia picked up a broom.

Everyone helped clean up the mess.

Even Randy the Robot was lending a claw.

"Amelia Bedelia," said Miss Edwards.

"Do not be so hard on yourself.

Many scientific breakthroughs

are made by accidents and mistakes."

"In that case," said Amelia Bedelia,

"I should get two Nobel Prizes:

one for blowing the volcano's top,

and one for blowing Dr. Dinglebatt's top."

They had just finished cleaning up

when the gym door flew open.

"Eureka!" shouted Dr. Dinglebatt.

"I found it, I found it!"

"I take it back," said Amelia Bedelia.

"He is happy he found his hair."

"Are you still a mad scientist?"

asked Artie.

"Mad?" said Dr. Dinglebatt.

"I am not a mad man.

I am a happy man!"

"That's a switch,"

said Miss Edwards.

"Precisely," said Dr. Dinglebatt.

"Back at my lab, I was inspired

to improve my latest invention.

I switched a switch,

added a little surprise,

and here it is."

"We've got one of those," said Jason.

"It is a TV remote control."

"That's right," said Dr. Dinglebatt.

"But this remote control can never get lost."

"My dad needs one of those," said Artie.

"Everyone does," said Wendy.

"How does it work?"

"Clap your hands," said Dr. Dinglebatt.

"Look familiar?" said Dr. Dinglebatt.

"I call it my Tip-Top Remote.

It blows its top before you blow yours!

And I am giving half of the credit to a

rocket scientist named Amelia Bedelia."

"That is terrific," said Miss Edwards.

"Thanks for coming back to show us."

"Actually," said Dr. Dinglebatt,

"I came back to apologize.

I am sorry I lost my temper."

"No harm done," said Amelia Bedelia.

"I am glad," said Dr. Dinglebatt.

"In fact, I will recommend

that my university

sponsor your fair from now on."

"Hooray," shouted the children.

"Wonderful," said Miss Edwards.

They were still clapping and cheering

when Mr. Rogers walked in.

"Thank you!" said Mr. Rogers.

"It is nice to feel appreciated."

"Stop dreaming," said Amelia Bedelia.

"We are not clapping for you."

"You should," said Mr. Rogers.

"I brought in your science project."

"My what?" said Amelia Bedelia.

"Don't be modest," said Miss Edwards.

"Aha!" said Dr. Dinglebatt.

"You really are a rocket scientist."

"No," said Mr. Rogers. "I was wrong.

Amelia Bedelia is actually a chemist."

"I am?" said Amelia Bedelia.

"You bet," said Mr. Rogers.

"Here is her secret formula:

Combine citric acid, H_2O, cornstarch,

sucrose, and a pinch of sodium chloride.

Pour it into a pan lined with ground wheat.

Cover with protein. Heat to 350 degrees.

When the top turns brown, it's done."

"That is incredible," said Miss Edwards.

"Sounds edible," said Dr. Dinglebatt.

"I sure hope so," said Amelia Bedelia.

"It is my recipe for lemon meringue pie.

I made pies for my fellow scientists."

"And here they are," said Mr. Rogers.

"You left these pies behind this morning."

"Amelia Bedelia," said Dr. Dinglebatt,

"you are an amazing cook."

"Amazing what?" said Amelia Bedelia.

"I mean," said Dr. Dinglebatt,

"you are an amazing chemist.

I have just one word for your pie."

"DELICIOUS?"

said Mr. Rogers.

"YUMMY?"

said Miss Edwards.

"MORE?"

said Amelia Bedelia.

Dr. Dinglebatt pointed at his pie

and shouted: "Eureka!"